I0672963

1

I Longed for *Love*,
I Found *Madness*

ISBN: 978-1-962072-18-2
Cover art & design by: Mitch Green

Octave
Eight
PUBLISHING
∞

octaveeightpublishing@gmail.com
www.octaveeightpublishing.com

ACKNOWLEDGMENTS:

To my family, I love you so much.
Life is beautiful with all of you in it.
Thank you for it all.

Dedicated to all those who find themselves
truly, madly, deeply, in love.
This is for **you.**

""""Be with me always. Take any form. Drive me mad! Only do not leave me in this abyss, where I cannot find you! Oh, God! It is unutterable! I can not live without my life! I can not live without my soul!"

— Emily Brontë, Wuthering Heights

let the world slip away,

let our chaos ignite.

for loving you, darling,

is a perilous race.

but in this wild love,

i find my true light.

i am what nightmares are made of.
i promise you'll fall in love quick.
i'm excitement, thrill, and adventure,
all for your mind to twist.
i'll leave you climbing death valley
all to feel my thrill once more,
while everyone asks if you went crazy —
acting so out of character.
i'm the ride of a lifetime —
the sacred lust you've been trying to find.
the dark one
you are craving at least one more time.

keep an eye out for the girl the gods fear.
in her eyes, a flicker of ancient stars.
you notice right away, as they help heal
your scars.

she holds secrets to the universe within her core,
she felt you begging for more.
she is your paradox of chaos and calm.
she's the storm and the calm before it's psalm.

be wise with her heart.
she can make you feel ecstasy
or she can sink you into hell.
she's a force to be reckoned with,
by all above and below.

her love though, is also rare and true —
be good to her,
and she'll do anything for you.

forget him.

how do you forget part of yourself?
because he is as much me as i am him.
you could lobotomize me and still
my mind and heart will remember him.
so, no, i can't, no matter what anyone
says or does.
he's now my sanity,
and i'm losing myself in his touch.

they said sexually transmitted demons
weren't real, yet here i am trying to exorcise
the last of you off me,
sadly knowing i can't.
and tonight i'll just grow another attachment
until they take over me.
all over *loving* you.
i can tasted the other girls off you,
as i do the nicotine.
and knowing my fate, i still choose you.
maybe it makes me crazy.
but aren't we all a little mad?

as i trace the lines of your smile in the dark,
and feel the rhythm of your heart
mapping the routes of our fevered embrace,
you are the tether, the anchor, and the gale.
my tempest of passion.
to love you fiercely, i teeter.
i sail on the brink of my sanity,
wild and free
all because of thee.

loving you was suicide.

quicker than the moon pulls the tied,

i was dead to you.

they spoke of you,

they said your charm was gilded lace,

a velvet trap,

a false embrace.

and though your voice was soft and kind,

they warned me of your darkened mind.

they spoke of hearts you left in shreds,

of broken dreams and tangled threads.

yet still i wondered, could it be,

that he was more than what they see?

for in your gaze,

a mystery,

a promise masked like history.

and though they spoke of heartache dire,

i felt a spark,

i felt an all consuming fire.

i'm the clown with the sorrowful face,

in the circus of a fickle place.

my painted smile,

a mask i wear,

hiding the hear that's laid bare.

beneath the laughter,

hidden tears echo the whispers

of my fears.

in the spotlight's fleeting grace,

i hide the ache that time won't erase.

"whore," they spit with venom and disdain,

a scarlett letter etched upon my name.

judgment forged from society's gaze.

chains of shame in their relentless maze.

but i am more than words thrown in spite,

beyond their narrow, blinded sight.

i am flesh and spirit, fire and grace,

not defined by their misplaced disgrace.

the warmth we shared now fades away,

replaced by the cold of disarray.

in the silence, i hear the cries

of a love that's gone and left no goodbyes.

in the chamber of my fractured mind,

where echoes of lost love unwind,

madness whispers through the air,

as memories turn to dark despair.

your name a haunting,

a cruel refrain,

a ghostly presence in my brain.

each thought, a sharp and twisting knife,

wounding the remnants of my life.

i chase the shadows of your smile,

lost in madness all the while.

the world distorts in pain and rage,

as i unravel page by page.

the days blend into a ceaseless storm,

where sanity and sorrow both form.

a tempest of the heart's dismay,

that sweeps my reason far away.

yet in the chaos, faintly seen,

a glimmer of what might have been.

and though my mind is torn and frayed,
love's ghost will dance in *madness* made.

they spoke of me as foolish

for believing in something as sacred as you.

and i think them stupid for being so naive,

telling me i couldn't be part of you.

they tried to deny our souls were interwoven,

yet still they looked up at the stars in awe.

i call them hypocrites.

we are as endless as the night sky they stare at.

a timeless tale.

and one day they will bite their tongues

as they stare upon the magic we create.

for in your ignorance,

you fail to see the depth of my soul

and how truth will set me free.

my worth is not measured by your cruel score.

i will rise above. i am not your whore.

in defiance, i reclaim my own voice,

no longer shackled by your shallow choice.

i am strength and resilience,

fierce,

and truth unveiling scars to the light,

breaking through.

so cast your stones and name me what you will.

i rise, unbroken, rising higher still.

for in the face of judgement,

i find my power.

no longer silenced by your shaming hour.

lies spun like silk to inflict stain.

"what a slut," they chant,

with a cruel degree.

but your words, like daggers,

won't define me.

i am not the names you hurl in hate,

nor the judgements that seal my fate.

i can be a "bitch," and you'll see soon,

your skeletons will come out dancing

your secrets too.

i gave my naked body to you

then after you got what you wanted

decided we were through.

blocked from your world,

a digital divide.

where i thought love thrived,

pain now resides.

your absence is a void

as i scream silently

there are too many words left unspoken,

too many things left unsaid —

like why you hurt me this bad

for just a night in your bed.

but i'll let go,

i release you with a whispered sigh,

in a space where love and sorrow lie.

i was blocked but not broken.

tear soaked, i will remember as i shed you off my skin, and onto my alter. you will never again make a woman falter. you played a dangerous game, *with the wrong witch.*

when we return to bones
may you never leave me alone.
while our souls resurrect
holding hands, as we walk into the next life,
where we find one another again, in love.
and one day walk past the tombstone
of whom we use to be with faint familiarity.

as we read amongst their tombstones,
"their souls will always be one,"
may our love stay cursed to this earth
to never be undone.

one day, this twisted mind of mine
will turn into nothing but a skull
that was once full of dreams i never
got to fulfill,
because of a love that was taken from me
too soon.
as my skull lay broken and bruised,
withering to dust,
may my soul find yours as we dance
under the moonlight
rejoined in lust.

drive me to the brink of insanity,

then stop.

pull me back into your arms.

kiss me and don't cease til' death.

because the only joy i will ever find

is upon your lips.

a dance on edges, a perilous game,
in love's wild rush, we risk the flame.

    — *it's time to blow out our candle.*

we came together in madness

and loved so intensely

you brought me to insanity.

but all the greatest love stories

end in tragedy.

would we remember

romeo and juliet

if juliet didn't reject being a capulet,

and together they didn't take

the ultimate sacrifice?

they were just a boy and a girl

doing whatever they could to be together,

jus as i will do for you, forever.

like the lightening we create,
igniting our night,
in the dance of our laughter,
finally, everything feels right.
the clatter of moments,
unplanned and divine.
tangled sheets in the morning,
your hand entwined with mine.
colors bleed together,
a cannas unframed.
in the mess of our feelings,
we're *beautifully* untamed.

i taste your lips.

what a staggering twist.

your lips leave an aftertaste

i will now always crave.

while i breathe in your beauty,

you have become my favorite

october obsession.

let the world spin madly,
let the stars dance above,
for within this sweet
turmoil *lies the essence of love.*

you saw me down to my soul, naked and bare.

you taught me all the fucked-up things

that happened to me

to get to you were fair.

fair in a way that each bad moment of my past

just slipped away,

as if it never even happened.

all that was left in my mind was you.

someone to love me completely.

fully accept every flaw.

something i thought i'd never see in this lifetime,

you showed me.

i saw a man take a girl and love her broken

pieces back to life.

they all called me crazy for believing in you,

yet they turn to the sky and believe in things unseen.

from angels to aliens,

but when you speak of true love,

it's like taboo.

only something a select few get to experience.

but for you, i was told to give up my search and beliefs.

like a soul has faith in its maker,

i knew with the same certainty

my other half to my soul was coming home to me soon.

i didn't need to see you to know you were out there.

i felt you.

i just needed to wait.

chase me like michael myers.

leave me screaming at the fact

i cannot escape you.

leave me eternally running from

a passion so strong i have nowhere to hide,

but to face my monsters once, and for all.

leave me staring in the dark eyes i hid from,

yet my heart yearned to be caged in your madnesss.

i'd never thrive anywhere else.

this intense, toxic love is what sparks my soul.

i can never do a day mundane.

let's share our nightmares as we allow

our demons to dance to this toxic fate.

i know what you did last summer,

and i don't need a scary movie to tell,

because this small town knows

all the indiscretions you didn't hide so well.

they will come to haunt you,

one loveless lie at a time.

it's karmic how your phone rings

as i walk away

and hear you say, "who's this?"

don't come crying to me because

your demons catch up to you.

you thought yourself as "the man,"
because of how many broken hearts you left behind.
i think of you as a serial killer
who left a trail of victims leading right to you.
you thought you were tough.
you weren't.
there was just an insecure little boy
hiding in the flesh of a man.

you might not be trialed in this life
for the knives you left in so many backs,
but you will atone your sins
when you see the punishment awaiting
from our maker.

you are magic down to the very cells
that devoured your body.
people long to be near you,
and always gravitate straight to you,
without question.
like a moth to a flame,
you shine differently.
i crave your presence.
your soul heals mine.
your laugh is contagious.
your smile, it brings me to my knees.
your soul is beautiful.

i'll say it once more,
you are pure fucking magic —
perfect in every form.

we didn't fit in this world,

but we fit together.

we spoke a language crafted for us two.

a perfect amount of perpetual peculiar.

we were undeniably created for each other.

our love alone will make a difference.

it'll be proof there is still love left

in this cruel world.

let's play a game, where i lose myself
finding you. where i travel the intertwined
roads in your mind.
where i camp in the darkest part of your head,
all to bring you back to the light.
and as i walk this long-shadowed path next to you,
i grow fond of the quietness and find me
making a home in the madness you embody.

because after making love in the dark,
i don't see the light the same anymore.

go ahead, choose her,

the girl who spent thousands on surgery

and lip injections to look nothing like she would.

who thinks the real luxuries in life money could

buy.

it's only you who is punishing yourself,

when you realize you are laying in bed

next to someone so shallow.

it's sad you let your demons win.

she was momentary arm candy

for you to feed your ego.

was she perfect?

no — not at all.

did she look it?

yes.

was i jealous secretly?

yes.

not for her looks, but because

she had you.

and maybe if i looked like that,

i would too.

though they say love is blind,

i find it's anything but blind.

it's superficial and visual.

men are vile creatures,

parading around in beautiful bodies

choosing barbies over brains.

so how do i compete with that?

i can't, so i don't.

but how i crave for you to look at me that way.

the moment we met,

everyone was talking,

but it was pure silence to me.

i couldn't hear a sound,

and reality became wavy —

like heat in the desert, rising,

distorting my view.

i was losing consciousness,

then you spoke.

you only say "hey."

i then saw the sweat dripping from your forehead

and realized, you felt it too.

it was our souls merging.

it was that moment, an instant of my whole life,

that suddenly you became my entire existence.

i gave way too many fucks when i was younger.
spent my youth crying over pretend lovers,
just to have them at my knees when i was older.
one even get my name tattooed on his shoulder.
that poor sad girl,
she grows up to be a trophy, but not a wife.
she built her own empire and chased
her dreams and desires.
this is how a legend was made.

pretty please, be mine.

lets dance

under the black sky.

drive me mad.

i've got it bad for you.

drive me insane,

then blame it on the alcohol.

ruin my life.

it'll suck without you.

their tongues are sharp.

their eyes so cold,

casting stones from pedestals old.

in their rigid sanctums,

i am religiously shamed,

cast under their gaze,

because i chose to sacrifice my sanity

as i gave myself up sacrilegiously

as an offering to you —

beautiful you.

i worship you, yet wish no retribution

from the eyes that watch me

as i fall from grace.

but damn me, if you must.

his lips taste like redemption.

as a child, i feared clowns,
then i grew up and met you —
a clown parading around
in the most perfect body.
a disguise you wore too well.
you left me searching for that red balloon,
ready to be eaten alive.

our story was so cliché,

what can i say.

i think normal is boring.

so, i shook up the ending

and when you thought you broke my heart,

i left smiling.

you left crying,

begging to go back to the start.

you should have believed me

when i said, *i'm what nightmares are made of.*

now i won't lose a wink of sleep,

but you,

i'll haunt your mind til' you die.

as i lay crying at your feet,

begging you not to go,

you looked me dead in the eyes and said,

"i don't care, let go."

may the devil weep at your ignorance,

and your words come back to haunt you

for having someone fall so hard in love,

then rip it away for no reason at all.

i thought love was my cure,

but it was my downfall.

i learned to love is to possibly lose.

and it haunted my subconscious though.

like a succubus, the thought of being with you,

intoxicating.

so alluring, the beauty of our bodies together

haunted my dreams,

but i was played with fear.

i lost a love once. i can't succumb to that again.

yet i'm ready to end it all for you.

down the cliff i fall, arms wide open, into you.

and if you left me with anything,

it's that in the devastation you left behind

hid a madness that was unimaginably damaging,

yet beautiful, simultaneously.

poetic and painful, in the grievance

was left a muse.

and you smiled knowing it'd *always be you.*

your sacrificial stare made me
reject my religion.
i will be swallowed into darkness
if you're with me.
put a crown upon my head.
let me reign against your enemies.
i'll be your queen of devilry.
because those eyes,
as i stare,
they bring me to my knees.

i have been judged by so many
for far worse than who i chose to love.
so, when you ask me,
what do you think people will say,
i truly don't care. let them stare and snare.
you're too perfect to pass up,
especially when i'm already marked as
the outcast, and the black sheep of my family.

you mock me with a kiss.

those dark eyes, i've missed.

i was trying to be a saint,

but here you go making me a sinner.

as i ask,

"why do you only come to me at night?"

i realize, to you, i'm not love, only desire.

as you sire me to my knees

in flames of passion, i'm seized.

tell me your deepest secrets —

the ones that are hard to roll off your tongue.

your intimate desires and dark thoughts.

and watch me love you more.

don't be scared. i'll protect each secret

as my own.

let me know all of you,

from the vile, to the wickedness

you hold inside,

and let me love you anyway.

there's an icebox where your hear used to be.
chilled memories wrapped in frost,
and silent echoes of what used to be.
a warmth, forever lost.

i knew i'd rue the day you pushed me away,

even more so, the day we met.

i should have walked away.

i knew better,

yet i fell into madness with you.

the excitement was mistaken for love

and the feeling i thought was love,

was lust.

i mistook the way your hands slipped down my
body

for romance, when it was blasphemy you spoke,

and i naively reciting each line like it was the bible.

haunt me.

i beg of you.

scream my name,

and leave min a cold sweat.

just let me hear you.

people try and tell me i dodged a bullet

when you left.

no, i more so took one, straight through the heart.

over a love i was promised would last forever,

now it feels like forever since i've felt you.

so i'll close my eyes to find you in my nightmares,

waiting to terrorize me.

but oh, how handsome you look.

yet when morning comes,

i wake up and lose you all over again.

i feel a breeze as i'm wrapped in your arms.

how twisted it is that we shall fall in love

during the season everything around us is dying.

yet we come alive, and i find it utterly beautiful.

as the leaves fall, i fall deeply, madly, in love with you.

where i went wrong was trying to find you
when you didn't want to be found.
i had the naive notion that you cared.
i was wrong.
shame on me for being so gullible.
i made you into a hero,
when you were *just a wimp.*

i never expected to be your first.

i knew it would be a treacherous journey to you.

i even knew i wouldn't have you for long,

but the time we did have was going to be

soul shifting.

and it was nothing less than messrizing.

you made it that.

if today was my last,

i'd smile and say i lived because

i got to love you so intensely.

i saged myself.

as soon as you left

i felt the lies painting goosebumps

upon my skin, as you spoke them.

i couldn't wait for you to leave,

to wash the deceit off my body.

i said goodbye as i blew the smoke

all around me.

may i be cleansed of you and

your negative energy.

come join this hayride. it's haunted.
you'll see it haunted by memories of
my ex and me.
see, we sat right there, while he whispered
sweet nothings into the air.
words he didn't keep as promised,
yet still i ride this tractor and close my eyes,
to see those promises in the wind.
because *it's all i have.*

you took your time with me.

you knew i went through a lot.

the past relationships were unkind.

you put band-aids over my wounds

and you were considerate in all you did.

you thought of me and how i'd feel.

i never experienced that before.

your consideration was the highest form

of respect, in my eyes.

so, if you're reading this,

i want you to know, you hold a special

place in my heart,

and i'm grateful.

when you think of yourself,

you also think of me too. *i love you.*

i've tried to forget you,

but every time the noose

just got tighter.

i couldn't let you go,

and i couldn't stay.

i needed you like i needed my blood to flow

back to my brain.

i wish you'd loosen this noose,

and help me let you go.

or maybe i'm still just disheveled

from the lack of circulation.

you prove to me repeatedly,

i can't be without you.

but sometimes i just need to breathe —

but i need to breathe next to you.

life started feeling like solitary confinement,
then there you were, igniting my hope, bringing
back excitement to my life.
the day you held my hand, my faith was restored.

with you, the world's hues are so much clearer.
you made it so that when i look in the mirror,
i see the beauty you see.

i have never favored fairytales.

i never truly believed in a happy ending.

there's something beautiful about a love

so tragic it breaks you down to your very core,

craving to have more.

a love so strong it reaches through realms and

is recognized each lifetime.

maybe that's why i always chased disaster.

subconsciously looking for that love

that's too strong for this world.

and then, uncoincidentally, i found you.

you would hide away.

i always thought it was me

that did something wrong,

or maybe i loved you more

and you just needed space.

it wasn't til' later

i realized your distance

was a silent confession of pain.

that's the moment i realize it

doesn't matter if our souls are tethered

or we are connected by an invisible string.

just being in love doesn't always take the pain

away.

you suffer in life,

even when surrounded by good.

pain doesn't discriminate.

though we were better together,

i wasn't ignorant anymore to the fact

soulmates can suffer too, and the best thing

i could do for you was make you know,

you are never alone… even if you felt it.

it was in the moments when i was with you,

my soul felt at peace.

your energy relaxed me.

when we were together, the world was quiet,

and i felt calm.

it was every one of these moments,

in silence, alone together, i realized being with you

was the calm i couldn't find anywhere else —

the calm i craved and needed so badly.

i was safe with you.

your words were simple,

yet they carried the weight of the world.

"i'll do my best for you."

it came out so effortlessly.

i understood how much you truly wanted too,

but your words carried too much promise

and your actions didn't speak the same language.

you tried.

you tried hard, and i'm grateful you chose to carry

that weight for me, but you didn't realize

i was always

there holding up your burdens as if

they were my own.

you never walked alone.

you said we'd need a miracle,

but the miracle was always you.

when i close my eyes for the last time,

promise when they open,

you'll be there standing before me.

because i know this life we are in has uncertainties,

but the one thing i am completely certain of is,

if it's not you, with no goodbyes,

then it can't be the heaven i prayed for.

you and i, we went past any superficial attraction.
it was real, raw, and emotional.
so emotional it brought me to tears, but in
happiness,
over the small things we got to share.
we respected each other and trusted one another
with anything. but the way i truly knew we cared
for each other was the way we loved *without*
expectations.
we loved *naturally, effortlessly,* and it was *beautiful.*

i cannot fathom a day without you.

i'd rather drown in the dead sea then be

without you for a moment.

i love you.

so if your fate dances with death and you're taken,

back into the soil, i'll willingly go too.

because you are my existence, my favorite type

of madness. *and i can't be without you.*

the world would become too mundane.

one minute, things seem okay.

then the next, i'm digging up old videos

from our beginning, just to hear your voice.

i still can't accept there was an end to such a

beautiful story.

we should have been the greatest trilogy ever told

—

not just a chapter.

what i have come to realize on this journey,

is most people are not going to understand me or my

pain, and that's okay.

but i'm going to feel it anyway.

my soul is growing and changing.

there are moments i feel empty and moments i feel

whole, but in both moments, til' my last breath,

i will forever be grieving you.

truly,

madly,

deeply.

you've stolen the heart from inside me,

put it on a plate and served it as

your favorite meal,

all because i loved you too much,

and you only wanted to feel my tough —

blood dripping from your chin,

even then, you're beautiful.

what an intangible lesson i had to learn,

because you wanted to eat alone.

i always knew what i brought to the table,

i just never though i'd lose it all in you.

some people sleep soundly with arms around them,
while others are hugging the pillow, crying over the
arms that once held them tight.
i'm nothing like them.
i stay up late, reminiscing.
i have a nostalgia i'm never going to be able to let go
of. your memory, it's such a beautiful reel i replay.
and as my eyes grow tired, i speak out loud, "come to
my dreams."
that's now our hide away — in my mind;
the only happiness i find.

you were my fatal flaw,

wrapped in a red bow.

you came to me gifted by the gods.

you were perfect.

what are the odds, that they'd gift me you,

except what i always knew —

the gods make monsters too.

it must be a cruel joke.

it can't be true.

i can't understand why,

if i gave my entire being to you,

you'd do something to jeopardize

killing our soul.

you said we were one,

together forever.

now it's me, here alone.

i can't fathom or accept it,

but part of me knows it's true.

our story is through, too soon.

i used to believe all roads in the world would
always lead me to you, but roads crack and get
covered in snow, or asphalt burns.
i sadly learned, not all roads are always travel able,
and the road to get to you now
has been ripped away.
you travel a road i can't get to.
i'll still try through dreams of you.
i now walk alone, but never stop remembering you.

you're my heart, and my soul.

and while that has been said so many times,

it now feels insignificant to repeat,

but i was awoken the moment i met you

for the first time.

i was truly living in the moment.

i saw the colors — vibrant, clear.

and while i may get weak for you,

there's nothing else in the world that

could make me feel as alive as you.

you may bring me to my knees in madness,

but you also are my only cure

to bring me back from the confines of my mind.

i loved you in a way that if

you needed me, i'd drop everything.

as it shattered onto the floor, i'd run

across the debris, cutting my own feet.

i'd crawl to you, if need be.

bleeding as i rushed to get to you,

i'd find a way, even, to run,

but i'd get to you as fast as i could.

— *i'd get to you.*

i may have grown and put away my childish things,
but our love keeps me young. even with all the stress
and responsibilities i carry daily,
i still believe your kiss can heal my wounds,
and that i'm safe at night, next to you.
that you'll rid the monsters from the closet.
there is an innocence about our love.
it's like we are both two children learning the world,
protecting each other.
and i find the beauty in that —
maybe, we are being for each other,
what we always needed as kids.

i sometimes wonder what it was about you
that made me hold on so tightly.
i was so used to people coming and going.
maybe it was the way i craved a love as
deep as the ocean, and you engulfed me
into the endless black abyss —
our first kiss.

it took time for us to get to know each other,

though our souls knew each other right away,

our bodies, and minds took the time to learn

each detail —

your likes, your dislikes,

your wants, and your needs.

before we intimately knew each other,

we mentally knew one another.

i saw your mind naked before i saw your body.

we knew one another deeply,

inside and out.

i knew your fears, and you knew mine.

i knew what would make your eyes shine.

and that's when i knew — you were my king,

and i'd always be your queen.

this was our beautiful fairytale,

(but even fairytales end.)

i used to think social media was useless,

that it was only people craving attention.

then i became *that* person, only craving you.

i met you, and soon after, i started taking selfies,

hoping you'd think i was pretty.

i was so naive, because you already did.

you were home saying,

"she's so beautiful, she'll never fall for me."

"oh, my sweet boy, i already did."

still i'd write statuses about things you liked.

post a meme about love, looking for your

heart's reaction. i would bypass every like or

comment, only searching for your name.

it wasn't the internet's approval i was searching for.

it was always yours. each post was an encrypted

message of love. every song was to you. every lyric

was everything i was too shy to say. long story short

we ended up together in the end.

you might just be the death of me —
the ravenous monster that has come to
leave me screaming.
but i invited you in and i don't think i mind,
as you whisper, "are you afraid of the dark?"
i smile as i pull the curtains closed.

when i finally leave you'll be free
from all solicitation from me.
i will no longer drag myself across
embers to try to sell my love
to undeserving eyes.
no, the witch doesn't burn in this story,
over a love not meant for her.
instead i will raise the dead and spark
these embers into a raging fire
that will give you no chance
but to notice me there.
i will be no damsel in distress,
but i will leave you feeling
a fire inside you can't ignore.

burn me, stone me, lash me.

do whatever you must.

you have already taken all of me.

you wanted to know what loyalty

felt like. well loyalty is me here on

this metaphorical cross, devoting myself to you.

what more can i do, than take nothing less than the

ultimate sacrifice for you.

i hope now you see what someone truly devoted

to you will go through.

that's loyalty, or maybe stupidity.

there's a fine line between both when it comes

to what i'd do for you.

i never needed protection from your lies,

but one day, when they become too much

for me to hear, you will need protecting from me.

so before you go and tell another lie,

whisper, "god save my soul," because i will show

no mercy. this is the monster you created.

to the one who hurt me,

especially the one who always claimed,

"never my son,"

may you live with the anguish

i had to feel when i tried to save him,

and you babied him to death.

sometimes we aren't meant to get over someone.
that's a lesson in life i've learned to be cruel —
that we must go on living a bit emptier,
with our hearts a bit heavier.
sometimes we must go on loving someone,
without them.
you taught me that soulmates do exist,
but not everyone gets to keep theirs —
that the faith i had in fairytales wasn't fair.

you taught me it's more beautiful to have
loved and lost,
than to have never loved at all.
but, going on without you,
i'm never going to be whole again.

i have all my crystals in a circle under
the full moon. they said doing this with the
intentions of being with you
can bring you back to me.
so while i manifest you here, and my crystals are
powered by the universe,
may you miss me as i miss you.

you thought of me as a sheep,

but i ran the lion's den.

so, when you tried to pull one over on me,

you soon learned i'll eat your heart out

if you mess with my pride or think of me

as weak, just because i'm a girl —

no, i'll eat you alive with a smile.

i won't lose sleep.

i wish you were here still underneath

the same sky.

but your sky shines endless white day and night,

and mine right now is black.

i like to think you're somewhere so beautiful that

words couldn't even express the magnificence.

but part of me is selfish and wishes you were still here,

even if it's as a ghost.

i need you in any form, to survive.

you are my before and after.

before we met, i dreamt of you, faceless.

i kissed your unseen lips a thousand times.

in dreams, i've held you.

then, there you were.

you became the moment everything changed.

because after, there was only you.

and now, can only ever be you.

even before we met, my soul would yearn

for you.

you were always everything, to me.

i am lost in the way i long for you,

but not lost in the way i feel for you.

my heart knows no distance

and my heart is yours.

it's longing for your touch,

it feels you out there, yet hasn't felt your flesh

in a while.

that's where the confusion lies.

my heart feels your soul, but my body

misses your touch.

it's been too long since i've felt you.

i miss you so much.

someone asked me about you,

and while i was so happy that

they brought you up,

they asked me to describe you, and i can't.

toy are too beautiful to explain in words.

so, i respond:

he's the night sky.

he's raw excitement and wonder.

he's a mystery to psychics.

he's something you don't expect coming.

he's colors to a blind person.

he's something you don't see, just feel.

he's the bible to christianity.

he was a story before there were even words to tell.

he is absolutely everything.

when the world set low expectations

on what to expect,

he came, and he made me believe in magic.

i never thought someone would

ever love me enough to marry me.

secretly i was so insecure and didn't think

me of all people would be lucky enough

to find such a grand love.

people would always say, "you're beautiful."

i just never felt it.

not until the day you said it,

then you were on your knees

with the ring i always dreamt of,

designed especially for me..

asking, "will you marry me" that day,

you made my insecurities go away,

and made all my dreams come true.

my prince charming did exist, *and he was you.*

these wilted roses i leave before you,

red like my hear you ripped out.

this is the funeral for my love,

and the chances you'll never get again.

they're now dead.

i remember what you said.

"you can never live without me."

so may you rest in peace.

you thought you left me for dead

the day you walked away, hand in hand with her.

but little did you know, i knew it was all a show.

you thought you were making me jealous,

but i was the one making a real connection.

so when you came back trying to play

the heartbroken victim, he was already holding

my heart and in my bed.

— *i hope it hurts*.

i wasn't a game for you to play.

now you know how fast the tables can turn.

there's no "faking it" with me.

i feel vibes.

so, when you smiled and said,

"no, i'd never do that, i love you,"

your words sent a shiver down my spine.

and while i usually like tragically

twisted men,

i don't like unfaithful ones.

time to say *goodbye.*

you had an arsonist heart

and i loved watching

the way our flames danced together

in conjunction with the wind.

the ground ignites as soon as my feet

hit the ground every morning.

and if you're not careful, the same thing

can happen to you.

be cautious with me.

i can move mountains.

i'll either be proof that destruction

can be beautiful,

or showy a tragically beautiful demise.

beneath her skin, rivers of untamed desire flow,

challenging fate, where boundaries dare not go.

she defies the heavens with each fearless stride.

a rebel soul, with passion as her guide,

and you by her side.

together, you are both unstoppable.

my self-wroth shouldn't feel
like an act of bravery.
the way you try to belittle me
with the same tongue you please
me with.
no sir, you don't get both
pleasure and pain out of me.

you were the ringmaster of the circus,

and i had front row seats to your show.

little did i know, i'd become part of your next act,

where you hypnotized me in love,

and unleash creatures in my mind.

what i thought was true love

was all a show, where you turned me from

the innocent girl, to the monster you now know.

juggling fire at a circus is impressive,
but have you ever juggled
multiple mental illnesses and went
about your day as if it was normal,
when your head was really a freak-show.

i unmasked my demons.

i let them show this is the me

you will now know.

engulfed in the pain,

i finally went insane.

so when you glance my way,

don't be surprised when hysteria

hits and i say, "i'm fine."

as i whisper with a grin,

"why so serious."

love drove me fucking delirious.

my life was a tragedy.

love destroyed me.

if i didn't laugh, i'd cry.

so instead, i turned my life into a comedy

because what doesn't break you only makes

you stronger, right?

no, it makes you stranger.

and love brought me to sadness,

 i then turned to madness.

i'd rather love you and be insane,

than be without you, in pain.

as i peel back the mask, you can now see
the real me — the untamed me, enchanted by
delirium. taunted by a love i traded for my sanity.
i'm not scared. i'm psyched i can finally be me,
in love with you, sitting back, clapping at their
judgement. they may hide their chaos,
but i engulfed myself in you, not caring about
the consequences.

i was your contortionist,
bending over backwards for your love.
metaphorically and quite literally.
only to learn you thought we were
"clowning around," and i was only
the side show, not the main act.

i saw a boy get off his motorcycle

and take off his helmet.

until the moment i saw his face,

i swore it was you.

my heart dropped and the few seconds it took him

to take off his gear felt like eternity.

it wasn't you. it couldn't be. i know that.

but my heart still cries out in hopes it will be.

but it's not. maybe i'm delusional, but i will,

with a heavy heart, always search for you.

my beautiful bad boy — oh, how i miss you.

fall darling, fall from grace.

they are going to judge you anyway.

at least this way they can't take

away your authenticity.

it's time to love being the black sheep

of the family.

you can be a rebel with a good heart —

never forget that.

like a leech, you drained me.

siphoning my light.

each whisper i turned to shadows;

each dream, consumed by night.

your laughter wrapped in silence.

a haunting, ghostly plea.

what once was sweet and vibrant,

now echoes, that haunt me.

all because, like a leech, you drained me.

i gave you all my colors,

a canvas wide and bare.

but with each fleeting moment,

you stripped away at my care.

now careless, i walk free

from what was never meant to be.

we stand, side by side.

two hearts entwined in this relentless tide.

through storms that rage, and whispers of doubt,

we fight to stay alive, refusing to bow out.

i'd rather the fragments of the hopes we've
amassed, holding them close, as shadows are cast.
for every scar worn, a story i will tell, of a love's
fierce endurance, of a miracle's spell.
together we'll wander through valleys of fear,
with dreams as our compass, our vision made clear.
in the fight for our lives, we find what is true.
i'll stay strong for me, and i'll fight for you.

it's not personal, but i hexed you.

a flick of the wrist, a whispered ado.

in shadows, i linger, where echoes reside.

just as a small reminder, i vex you inside.

your laughter once danced like light on this breeze,

now tangled in spells that bring you to your knees.

it's not personal, love. it's a curious phase.

for in the hex's grip, and vexing of hearts,

we find the strange beauty, where longing starts.

ABOUT THE AUTHOR:

Jessica Livia, also known as LIVV, is a poetry author, single mother, and widow. She believes in expressing herself through the magic of words. She writes to share with the world her belief that there is a such thing as love after death, for love never truly dies.

To keep up with the author,
follow her social media handles:

Instagram: @livv.poet
Tiktok: @livv.poet

Instagram: @octaveeightpublishing

Tiktok: @octaveeightpoetry

Email:
octaveeightpublishing@gmail.com

Website:
www.octaveeightpublishing.com